HENNY PENNY

story retold by Jim Lawrence • illustrated by Tim Hildebrandt

Modern Publishing
A Division of Unisystems, Inc.
New York, New York 10022

Henny Penny was pecking about in the barnyard one day, looking for corn.

She scratched here and there among the leaves under a shady oak tree. Sometimes she found tasty tidbits.

Just then a breeze ruffled the branches of the big oak. An acorn came loose and fell out of the tree.

Bonk! It hit Henny Penny right on the head.

"Awwwk! The sky is falling! The sky is falling!" cried Henny Penny.

She bustled out of the barnyard, cackling, *"Cluck, cluck, cluck, ka-dawk!* I must go tell the King!"

Henny Penny hustled and bustled along until she met Cocky Locky.

"Cock-a-doodle-doo! Where are you off to?" crowed Cocky Locky.

"The sky is falling!" clucked Henny Penny. "I must go tell the King!"

"*Urk-urk-kadurk!* May I go with you?" asked Cocky Locky.

"Of course, you may! Come along! But we must hurry!" she fussed. "The sky is falling!"

So they hustled and bustled, and hackled and cackled along until they came to Ducky Wucky.

"Here now, what's all this?" quacked Ducky Wucky. "Is something wrong?"

"Didn't you know? The sky is falling!" said Henny Penny and Cocky Locky. "We must go tell the King!"

Ducky Wucky flapped his wings and waddled about. *"Snick-snock-snack! Quack, quack, quack!* May I go with you?"

"Yes, yes, certainly you may!" said Henny Penny and Cocky Locky. "But there's no time to lose! The sky is falling!"

So they hustled and bustled, and hackled and cackled, and waddled and doddled, until they came to Goosey Loosey.

"Honk-honk! What's going on?" asked Goosey Loosey.

"The sky is falling! Haven't you heard?" said Henny Penny and Cocky Locky and Ducky Wucky. "We're going to tell the King!"

When Goosey Loosey heard the news, she fluttered and flapped her wings and stretched her neck. *"Hinkety-honk!* May I come along?" she asked.

"Yes, yes, come along! But hurry!" they said. "We must tell the King that the sky is falling!"

So they hustled and bustled, and hackled and cackled, and waddled and doddled, and hinked and honked, until they came to Turkey Lurkey.

"Where are you all going?" gobbled Turkey Lurkey.

"To tell the King the sky is falling!" said Henny Penny and Cocky Locky and Ducky Wucky and Goosey Loosey.

"*Hobble-gobble, wibble-wobble!* Then I'd better go, too!" said Turkey Lurkey.

So they hustled and bustled, and hackled and cackled, and waddled and doddled, and hinked and honked, and hobbled and gobbled—and suddenly they met Foxy Loxy.

"Dear me, why the rush?" asked Foxy Loxy. "Something important must be happening—right?"

"Oh, yes, indeed!" said Henny Penny and Cocky Locky and Ducky Wucky and Goosey Loosey and Turkey Lurkey. "The sky is falling! We're going to tell the King!"

"Good thinking!" said Foxy Loxy. "It's lucky we met, because I know a shortcut to the King's palace! Just follow me!"

So they did. And do you know where Foxy Loxy led them?

To his underground den!

"Right this way friends!" said Foxy Loxy as Henny Penny, Cocky Locky, Ducky Wucky, Goosey Loosey and Turkey Lurkey followed him through the narrow, dark passage that led there.

It became darker and darker as they were led farther and farther by the crafty fox. Henny Penny didn't like it one bit and she started to lag behind. As her friends disappeared into the tunnel, she became convinced that this wasn't the way to the King's palace.

So the scared little hen turned around and came hackling and cackling out of the darkness into the bright sunlight.